DEMCO

Firehorse Max

Sara London · pictures by Ann Arnold

MICHAEL DI CAPUA BOOKS · HARPERCOLLINS

For Dean
And in memory of my grandparents,
David and Yetta London,
whose tales of my great-grandfather,
Aaron Hillel London, planted the seeds of this story.
S. L.

For Aldo
and his grandparents
A.A.

In a small Vermont town lived a hardworking peddler named Grandpa Lev. Every day he harnessed Bubba to his wagon, then off they went to sell his goods. Simon and Yetty liked to ride along too.

"He's all the shops on Church Street put together!" people said as the wagon went clanking by.

One morning Bubba would not get up. "Grandpa," said Simon, "something's wrong with Bubba!" He pulled on her mane. Yetty tugged on her tail. But Bubba would not get up.

"Run and fetch Dr. Samuelson," said Grandpa Lev.

Dr. Samuelson looked in Bubba's eyes. He looked in her ears and ran his fingers along her teeth. "I'm afraid she's too old to be pulling that wagon around," he said.

"What good is a peddler without a horse?" said Grandpa Lev. "My poor Bubba." And he kissed her nose, right between her big pink nostrils.

"Who will bring me my feather pillows?" said Mrs. Gamboni.
"What about my new reading lamp?" said Mr. Sims.
"I won't go to the shops," Mrs. Frumpkin complained. "The prices are too high."

"Have you heard the news?" said Dr. Samuelson. "The firehouse has two brand-new engines, and all the firehorses will be auctioned. I'm off to tell the old peddler."

Simon and Yetty had never been to an auction.

"Now there's a clever horse," said Grandpa Lev. "He's nodding to the music."

"Maximilian just *loves* a good tune," said Mr. Hefflon, the fire chief. "Who would like to take him home?"

Maximilian stomped his hooves and swished his tail.

"I'll give you sixty," said Grandpa Lev.

"Sixty-one," said the blacksmith. "Sixty-two," said the milkman. "Sixty-three!" shouted Simon and Yetty.

"Whose bid was that?" said Mr. Hefflon.

Grandpa Lev looked down at his grandchildren. "Sixty-three it will be," he said.

"That's Firehorse Max!" said Brian O'Brien.
"Oh my," said Mrs. Gamboni.
"Thank heavens," said Mrs. Frumpkin.
"Splendid," said Mr. Sims.

"Bubba," said Yetty, "meet your new friend, Max. He's going to pull that heavy wagon for you."

"Max, you can tell Bubba about the big fires you put out," said Simon.

Simon and Yetty raced home from school the next day to help harness Max to the wagon. Max tugged this way and that and shook his head.

"Now, Maximilian," said Grandpa Lev, "I know putting out fires was exciting work. I had an exciting job once too—in the old country, I played in a famous orchestra." Max twitched his ears. "But now I'm a peddler, and together we're going to sell my goods."

"Come in, come in," said Mrs. Gamboni when she saw Grandpa Lev. "Oh, what lovely pillows!"

Just then fire bells began clanging in the distance. "Oh dear," she said. "But isn't it a fine thing we have new engines instead of those old horses?"

"Yes, indeed it is," said Grandpa Lev, and he headed back to his wagon.

But the wagon wasn't there!

"They went that way," said Brian O'Brien.

"Oh no!" said Grandpa Lev. *"Stop that horse!"*

Max galloped past the church and the butcher shop, the bakery and the library. The smell of smoke tickled his nostrils, and he ran faster and faster.

"Wait for Grandpa!" Yetty cried.

"You're not a firehorse anymore!" yelled Simon.

On Pine Street a burning warehouse filled the sky with dancing flames.

"This is madness!" said Grandpa Lev. "My goods are scattered all over town!"

Max hung his head low. He had reached the fire just as quickly as he could, but no one rubbed his side or scratched his chin.

As they walked home, a stranger handed Grandpa Lev a breadboard, two pots, and a straw hat. "I believe these belong to you," he said.

"I found a bat!" said Brian O'Brien.
Townspeople were picking up brooms, buckets, boots, and balls.
"Thank you," said Grandpa Lev. "Thank you all!"

"What a crazy day we had without you, Bubba, old girl," said Grandpa Lev.
Max looked at Bubba, and she rubbed her chin along his mane.

"Do you think Max misses putting out fires?" said Simon.

"I suppose he does," said Grandpa Lev. "But a tired old peddler shouldn't be chasing after a firehorse."

"Bubba can teach Max not to run away," said Yetty.

"Well then," said Grandpa Lev, "we'll take her along tomorrow."

But Max believed he had a job to do. He spun the wagon around and charged
back through town—past the church and the butcher shop, the bakery and the library.
He even passed a shiny red engine!

"False alarm," said Mr. Hefflon. "Maximilian, you're giving this peddler a very hard time."

"What are we going to do?" said Simon.

"We must think of something Max loves even more than putting out fires," said Grandpa Lev, "or he'll have to find a new job."

He scratched his beard. "Hmm," he said, "I just might have an idea."

The next night, as everyone lay sleeping, Grandpa Lev heard a loud whinny coming from the barn. Distant bells were clanging toward a fire.

He threw off the covers, pulled out his dusty violin, and dashed into the yard.

The barn doors burst open and out bolted Max!

Grandpa Lev began to play a lively melody, and Max snorted and reared. He raced toward the music, then toward the bells, kicking and tossing his mane.

And finally he turned and trotted back to Grandpa Lev, nodding his head up and down to the rhythm.

"Good fellow!" said Grandpa Lev, lifting his bow.

"Bravo!" shouted the neighbors. "Bravo!"

After that, Grandpa Lev brought along his violin whenever he peddled his goods, even though Max no longer paid much attention to the fire bells.

"There's the old peddler," the townspeople would say, "and there's Firehorse Max."

"What would they do without music!"